The Magic Lunch Box

by Hanna Kim • illustrated by Emily Paik

STONE ARCH BOOKS
a capstone imprint

Published by Stone Arch Books, an imprint of Capstone
1710 Roe Crest Drive, North Mankato, Minnesota 56003
capstonepub.com

Library of Congress Cataloging-in-Publication Data
Names: Kim, Hanna (Children's author), author. | Paik, Emily, illustrator.
Title: The magic lunch box / by Hanna Kim ; illustrated by Emily Paik.
Description: North Mankato, Minnesota : Stone Arch Books, an imprint of Capstone, [2024]
Series: Ben Lee | Audience: Ages 6 to 9. | Audience: Grades 2–3.
Summary: The first day of school in Michigan is a nightmare for Korean American fourth-grader Ben Lee, who grew up in Los Angeles surrounded by Korean stores and restaurants, but his new schoolmates laugh at the Korean delicacies he eats—until his unexpectedly magic lunch box teaches them all a lesson.
Identifiers: LCCN 2022044548 (print) | LCCN 2022044549 (ebook) | ISBN 9781669014409 (hardcover) | ISBN 9781669017578 (paperback) | ISBN 9781669017523 (pdf) | ISBN 9781669017547 (epub)
Subjects: LCSH: Korean American children—Juvenile fiction. | First day of school—Juvenile fiction. | Magic—Juvenile fiction. | Lunch boxes—Juvenile fiction. | Bullying—Juvenile fiction. | Michigan—Juvenile fiction. | CYAC: Korean Americans—Fiction. | First day of school—Fiction | Schools—Fiction. | Magic—Fiction. | Lunch boxes—Fiction. | Bullies and bullying—Fiction. | Michigan—Fiction. | LCGFT: Novels.
Classification: LCC PZ7.1.K57 Mag 2024 (print) | LCC PZ7.1.K57 (ebook) | DDC 813.6 [Fic]—dc23/eng/20221230
LC record available at https://lccn.loc.gov/2022044548
LC ebook record available at https://lccn.loc.gov/2022044549

Design Elements
Shutterstock: dawool

Designed by Jaime Willems

Printed and bound in China. PO5378

TABLE OF CONTENTS

CHAPTER 1

THE LUNCH BOX

Screech! The bus halted in front of me, and the doors flung open.

I hesitated, staring down at my new lunch box. Takion, the blue-and-white robot from my favorite Korean show, *Tobot V*, stared back at me from the front. On the opposite side, my mom had written my name—Ben Lee—in big, bold letters.

I hadn't wanted her to mess it up, but Mom had insisted. "What if you lose it?" she'd asked. "It's a new school. Better safe than sorry."

"Ummaaa," I'd groaned, using the Korean word for mom. We spoke both Korean and

English at home. "I'm in fourth grade. I'm not going to forget it!"

"C'mon, honey," Dad had said, giving Mom a hug. "Ben's responsible now, right?" He gave me a wink.

I'd nodded, but truthfully, I was nervous about starting a new school. Ever since Dad had announced his job was moving from California to Michigan, it had been one big change after another.

First, we'd packed up our apartment, right in the middle of Koreatown. It was surrounded by some of the best Korean shops, PC game rooms, and restaurants. It was the only neighborhood I'd ever known.

Then, Mom had been forced to sell *her* restaurant. It was one of the busiest in Koreatown. I'd loved visiting her there and stealing bites of food. I knew saying goodbye to it made her sad.

I'd been sad to leave behind my friends too, especially my best friend, Jaehyun. It didn't help that I was going to be a new student in January—smack dab in the middle of the school year. Everyone would already have friends to hang out with. I wouldn't know anyone.

What if Michigan kids don't like the same movies as the kids back in California? I'd worried. What if they don't play the same kind of sports? What if they don't even talk the same?

At least I had my cool *Tobot V* lunch box to show off. Mom had even packed kimbap—a Korean dish made with rice, veggies, meat, and pickled radish wrapped in seaweed—for my lunch.

Mom's kimbap ruled. It took her more than two hours to make and had ten different ingredients in it. It was my favorite food in the whole world!

"Getting on today?" a voice called, bringing me back to the present.

I looked up and saw the bus driver looking down at me.

I took a big, deep breath, nodded, and climbed up the bus steps. I studied the kids already in their seats. On my old bus, I would've sat up front with Jaehyun. We

would've spent the whole ride talking about the latest episode of *Tobot V*.

I sighed. I was really going to miss those talks. Now, I was too nervous to sit next to anyone.

Please let there be an empty seat, I thought as I made my way down the aisle. I finally spotted one in the corner at the back of the bus. *Whew!*

I sprinted toward the empty seat. Just as I sat down, I heard someone shout, "Wait! Wait!"

The bus doors flung open again. A boy dressed in head-to-toe soccer gear huffed and puffed his way onto the bus. He had a soccer ball tucked under his arm.

"I made it!" the boy exclaimed. With his free hand, he fist-bumped and high-fived almost everyone on his way by. "Hey! What's up, man? Hi, dude! Let's catch up during lunch."

The boy was short and skinny, but he walked down the aisle with the confidence of a celebrity greeting his fans. That made it extra surprising when he came to a stop right in front of me.

"Mind if I sit here?" he asked.

I nodded. "Sure."

He scooted next to me and put his soccer ball on his lap. "I'm Emilio," he said, offering his fist for a bump. "What's your name?"

I fist-bumped him back. "I'm Ben," I replied.

"I haven't seen you around. Are you new?" Emilio asked.

I nodded. "Yeah. This is my first day at Andaleen Elementary." Even saying the name of my new school aloud made my hands go sweaty again.

"What grade are you in?" he asked.

"Fourth," I answered. "You?"

"Fifth," Emilio said. He glanced down at my lunch box. "You like *Transformers*?"

My forehead wrinkled with confusion. "Huh?"

Emilio nudged his elbow toward my lap. "Your lunch box."

I looked down. "Oh, this is actually from *Tobot V*," I explained. "It's a Korean show. It's kind of like *Transformers*, though." I held up the lunch box for him to see.

Emilio nodded. "Cool! Maybe we can watch it sometime."

I was surprised. Emilio wanted to hang out with me? Maybe a new school wasn't so bad after all. Maybe Emilio would even become a new friend.

"That would be awesome," I said.

"Great! Sounds like a plan, Sam."

I wanted to remind Emilio that my name was Ben, but he'd already started talking to some of the other kids across the aisle.

I turned to look out the window and gulped. We'd arrived at school.

CHAPTER 2

THE KIMBAP DISASTER

I looked up at the tall brick school in front of me. All around me, kids raced past, saying hi to friends and talking about their weekends.

"Do you need help finding your classroom?" Emilio asked, shaking me out of my daze.

I didn't know where my classroom was, but I didn't want Emilio to think I was clueless.

"I'll be fine," I said casually.

"Okay! See you around." With that, Emilio took off, running to catch up with a group of his friends.

The second he left, I felt tiny. I reminded myself of the Korean proverb that Halmoni, my grandma, used to always tell me: "Even if you are cornered by a tiger, if you stay alert, you'll survive."

A new school wasn't exactly a tiger, but Halmoni had also explained what the proverb *really* meant. Even if you're in a scary situation, if you stay calm, everything will work out in the end.

Trying to look cool and confident, I took a deep breath and walked through the front door.

Inside, it didn't look too different from my old school. I walked past the cafeteria, the library, and lots and lots of classrooms. Other than the Michigan flag painted on one wall, everything felt familiar. That made me feel a little better.

I guess all schools are pretty much the same, I thought.

I pulled out the sticky note Mom had given me this morning. It had *3B*—my classroom—

written on it. Underneath, Mom had written *Hwaiting!* That meant "good luck" in Korean.

Room 3B, room 3B, room 3B, I repeated in my head.

I sped past crowds of kids until I saw a door with a label that said *3B*. Inside, a tall woman with blond hair and warm blue eyes stood near a desk at the front of the room.

"Hi, um . . . I'm Ben," I introduced myself. "It's my first day. I think this is my classroom?"

"Ben! Welcome!" the woman exclaimed, her eyes twinkling. "I've been expecting you. I'm Ms. Bailey, your teacher."

Other kids filed into the room too, catching up with each other and finding their seats. Some of them stared at me, probably wondering who I was.

When everyone had taken their seats, Ms. Bailey guided me to the front of the room. The other students turned to face me. Their stares felt like laser beams.

Oh, great, I groaned silently. The last thing I wanted to do was introduce myself to the class. I just wanted to sit in my seat like the other kids and blend in.

"Good morning, everyone!" Ms. Bailey began. "Let's all give a warm welcome to Ben. He's a new student here, and I know you'll all make him feel at home."

I waved awkwardly, hoping this moment would be over soon.

"Ben, you can have a seat in front of Shawn," Ms. Bailey said, pointing to a desk in the middle of the room.

I walked over to my desk, sat down, and looked up at the board. Ms. Bailey turned on a multiplication video. A moment later, I felt a tap on my shoulder and turned to see the boy behind me leaning forward.

"Hey! Ben, right?" he said.

"Yeah," I whispered as quietly as I could. I didn't want to get in trouble my first day at a new school.

"I'm Shawn. Where are you from?" he asked me.

"California," I whispered again, keeping an eye on Ms. Bailey.

"Cool!" he replied. "I went to California once! Did you live in Hollywood?"

I shook my head. I didn't even know if I had *ever* been to Hollywood. "No. I lived in Koreatown—in Los Angeles."

"Koreatown?" Shawn scrunched up his nose again. "Never heard of that."

I could feel my face getting red. Maybe I was stupid for thinking he would know about Koreatown. Maybe I should've just said I lived in Hollywood. That would've probably sounded cooler.

"Wait, aren't you from China, though? You look Chinese," Shawn added.

I froze. Why would he think I was Chinese? I was Korean. I had literally just told him I was from *Korea*town.

I sucked a breath in and quickly turned around to face forward. I ignored Shawn's attempts to regain my attention and instead focused as hard as I could on the video. So much for fitting in.

I spent the rest of the morning counting down the hours, minutes, and seconds until lunch. Finally, it was time to eat!

Ms. Bailey had us line up to go to the cafeteria. "I want everyone to walk quietly—let me repeat, *quietly*—to the door," she said.

We grabbed our lunches and fast-walked to the door. I bounced on my toes impatiently.

I couldn't wait to dig in to the kimbap waiting for me.

Ms. Bailey made her way to the front of our line. "Make sure to let Mr. Wiz pass by!" she called.

I peered around the kids in front of me to see a man with a long, wispy gray beard rolling a mop bucket down the hall toward us. He wore a black shirt and a pair of bright blue overalls.

"See you in the cafeteria, everyone!" Mr. Wiz said. He waved as he rolled past our classroom.

The other kids started chattering away again, but Mr. Wiz's eyes met mine for a brief second. He flashed me a toothy grin before continuing on his way.

Ms. Bailey led the way to the cafeteria. Inside, long rows of tables stretched across the room. I overheard bits of conversation as the other kids huddled with their friends.

"I think I might be the best soccer player on my team."

"Ally said she didn't want to be Erica's friend anymore!"

"Don't forget to meet us at the tree during recess!"

I looked around for a place to sit and fidgeted with my lunch box. At my old school, I'd always sat in the same seat at the same table with the same kids. Jaehyun and I spent the whole time talking about *Tobot V* or having a milk-bubble-making contest.

Here, I felt lost. I sat down at an empty table. Lunch was usually the best part of the day, but I could already tell it wasn't going to be as fun as I'd hoped.

A moment later, Shawn walked over with two other boys from our class. They sat down a few seats away from me. Shawn glanced up at me but then turned back and started talking with his friends.

I tried to ignore the pit in my stomach and focused on unzipping my lunch box. It almost felt like opening a Christmas present. I pulled out a red-capped container and took off the lid. The smell of yellow radish, beef, spinach, and pure goodness wafted to my nose.

Mmm. Kimbap.

"What's that?" a voice asked.

I glanced up. I'd been so focused on my lunch that I hadn't noticed Shawn moving closer. He was right next to me now. Well, more like half on top of me.

"Uh . . . it's kimbap," I replied.

"Kim-what?" he asked.

"Kimbap," I repeated.

"Kimb . . . yeah, whatever it's called. Is that your lunch?" he asked.

I nodded. "Yeah."

"Why is it black on the outside?" Shawn asked, scrunching his nose and pointing to my lunch.

"That's seaweed," I said.

"Seaweed?! You eat seaweed?!"

That's when my worst fear came to life. I didn't even know it was my worst fear until it happened.

A group of kids started crowding around me, staring and pointing at my lunch.

"What is that?"

"He said it's seaweed!"

"Why would he eat seaweed?"

"That smells weird."

"Is that even food?"

I glanced around at the other kids' lunches. At my old school, lots of kids brought Korean food for lunch: kimchi, kimbap, mandoo, bibimbap.

Here, everyone had sandwiches, chicken nuggets, or some other American food. My Korean lunch looked completely out of place.

"Y-yeah," I stammered. "I don't know why my mom packed this. It's gross."

I grabbed my lunch box, walked to the trash can, and threw the entire thing away. Then I sprinted straight for the bathroom.

CHAPTER 3

STALL NUMBER 3

P.U. I wish I had picked a different place to hide, but the bathroom was closest to the cafeteria. I pinched my nose, opened one of the stalls, and sat down.

I wasn't ready to go back. I could imagine the disgusted looks on the other kids' faces the second I stepped out of the bathroom. I *especially* didn't want to run into Shawn.

I covered my face with my hands. *I want to go back to California,* I thought.

I missed eating lunch with Jaehyun. I missed my usual spot in the cafeteria. Most of all, I missed not feeling alone. A tear rolled down my face, and I brushed it away with the sleeve of my shirt.

I thought back to the kimbap. Why did Mom have to pack me a Korean lunch? Didn't she know we weren't in Koreatown anymore? I was probably the only Korean kid in the whole school. Maybe the state! Okay, probably not the *entire* state. But it *was* different here.

"Ugh!" I shook my head as the bell rang, signaling the end of lunch. The more I thought about it, the more unfair it seemed. Why did we have to move? Why did I have to give up my friends? Why did *I* have to be the odd one out?

I clenched my hands into fists. "I wish I was like everyone else!"

Then I heard something strange—a loud *squeaaak*. The sound echoed against the bathroom walls. It sounded like creaky old wheels rolling across the tile floor.

I almost fell off the toilet seat. I hadn't seen anyone when I came into the bathroom.

"I-is anyone there?" I squeaked.

No answer. I peered through the thin crack of the stall door and saw a bright yellow glow. Moving slowly, I pushed open the door. The glow faded. In its place, there was nothing but an empty bathroom.

✦✦✦

I spent the whole bus ride home dreading going back to school the next day. Emilio waved for me to sit with him, but I just wanted to be alone. I couldn't stop thinking about what had happened at lunch. The comments. The pointing. The looks.

Even worse, when I'd finally gone back to the classroom—long after everyone else—Ms. Bailey asked what had happened. I'd lied and said I got lost coming back from the bathroom. Some of the kids had giggled, and a girl sitting near me had whispered, "The new kid is so weird!" to her friend.

As soon as the bus got to my stop, I bolted off and raced home. Mom was waiting for me.

"Ben! You're home!" She started firing off questions. "How was school? How is your teacher? Do you have homework? How are the kids? Did you make any friends? Oh! Did you—"

I tuned her out as I trudged across the living room. I threw my backpack on the floor and fell onto the couch. My stomach grumbled and growled. I'd almost forgotten about not eating lunch, but my stomach sure hadn't.

"Ben, did you hear me?" Mom asked. "I need your lunch box."

I froze. "Uh . . ."

Mom walked to the living room with her hands on her hips. "Don't tell me you left it at school," she said.

"Well . . ." I felt my face turn red.

"Did something happen?" Mom asked.

"No," I said quickly. "I just forgot it."

"Well, don't forget it tomorrow. That's a new lunch box! I hope you ate all your kimbap, or it's going to go bad."

"Yes, Umma," I answered.

I felt bad for throwing away my lunch. I knew my mom had to wake up early to make it fresh. I felt bad for lying to her too, but I didn't want to hurt her feelings.

"Hey, Umma?" I said. "Do you think you could you pack me a sandwich for lunch tomorrow?"

Mom looked confused. "Was something wrong with the kimbap?"

I shook my head. "No. I just . . . thought it might be easier for you to make than kimbap."

Mom smiled. "I don't mind. Without the restaurant, you and Dad are the only ones I have to cook for. Besides, we don't have any bread. Maybe I can pick some up at the grocery store next week."

Next week? I thought back to the other kids' faces when I'd opened my kimbap. A whole week of eating Korean food was *not* going to help me fit in. This day was going from bad to worse.

CHAPTER 4

THE SWITCH

"I know you wanted a sandwich," Mom said the next morning, "but I made you something better—mandoo! Your second favorite food in the world."

She proudly held out an open lunch box—my plain blue one from last year. Inside was a container full of handmade Korean dumplings, each one filled with shredded vegetables and ground pork.

I took it, barely holding in a groan. The food smelled delicious, but I was worried about what the kids would say about it at lunch.

"Thanks, Umma," I said. I zipped up the lunch box and lugged my things to the door.

"Jal-ga!" Mom called after me.

"Okay, see ya later!" I responded, slamming the door behind me.

I trudged down the street, feeling weighed down by the mandoo in my backpack. When I got on the bus, Emilio was waiting. He waved me over to the open seat next to him.

"Hey!" he greeted me. "You survived your first day."

I sat down and nodded. "Sure did."

"Ready for day two?" he asked.

"Yep!" I tried to smile, but it felt more like a grimace. "Super ready."

"Are you sure? You don't look very excited," Emilio said.

I hesitated for a minute. I didn't want to relive yesterday. But Emilio seemed like he cared.

"Well . . . something did happen yester—"

Just then, a kid in the seat across from me pinched his nose. "Ew! What's that smell? Something smells rotten." He looked in my direction, and I knew he was talking about my mandoo.

"What are you talking about? I don't smell anything bad," Emilio said.

I sank down in my seat. Yesterday I couldn't wait for lunch, but today I hoped it never came.

✦✦✦

When I walked into the classroom, it felt like everyone was avoiding me.

They're probably calling me stinky seaweed kid behind my back, I thought miserably.

Even worse, halfway through the morning, Ms. Bailey called me over. "Ben, can you come here for a second?"

I put down my pencil. We were supposed to be writing in our journals, but the only things I'd managed to "write" were a couple of scribbles.

As I walked over to Ms. Bailey's desk, I noticed the custodian, Mr. Wiz, cleaning outside of the classroom. He danced as he cleaned, wiping sweat away with the back of his arm. He seemed to sense my staring because he looked up and waved. I gave him a quick half-smile.

"I just wanted to check up on you," my teacher said when I reached her desk. "I know it must be hard getting used to a new school and a new city. Is everything okay?"

"Yes . . . everything is fine," I replied. I must not have looked fine, though, because she looked concerned.

I'm not sure what made me say it. Maybe it was because Ms. Bailey looked like she really cared. Maybe I was just feeling extra miserable. Whatever the reason, I took a deep breath and blurted out, "The other kids thought my lunch was weird."

Ms. Bailey's eyes widened. "Oh, Ben. I'm sorry. I'm sure the other kids didn't mean to hurt your feelings, though."

What was I supposed to say to that? Whether they'd meant it or not, I felt terrible.

"I'll talk to the class today about being kind," Ms. Bailey continued. "It'll be a good lesson for everyone!" She patted my shoulder.

"Bu—" I stopped myself. What was the use? Ms. Bailey wouldn't understand anyway.

✦✦✦

At lunch, I looked around for the emptiest spot in the cafeteria. I was dreading opening my lunch box.

Why mandoo? I thought. *Why not some regular ol' lunch? I wish Umma packed me something—anything—else!*

"Hey, Ben! Want to sit with us today?" Angie, a girl from my class, called to me. She pointed to a group of kids sitting at one of the front tables.

I hid my lunch box behind my back, just in case. "No thanks," I mumbled as I hurried past. "I already have a spot."

I didn't have a spot, though, so I wandered around looking for one. I saw Emilio on the other side of the cafeteria. He noticed me and waved.

For a second, I thought about sitting by him. Emilio didn't seem like he would say anything about my lunch . . . but his friends would probably make fun of it. I waved back and quickly walked to a corner spot where he wouldn't see me.

Slam! I practically threw my lunch box down on the table. Then I looked around to make sure no one was watching. My hands trembled as I reached for the zipper, imagining the small, fried dumplings sitting neatly in a plastic container.

That's when I saw it—a strange yellow glow at the corner of my lunch box. It grew bigger and bigger until my whole lunch box lit up like a giant light bulb!

What. In. The. World?!

I looked left. I looked right. I tried to cover my lunch box with my arms. I tried to shove it in my shirt. I even thought about throwing it in the trash, but then I'd really have to explain myself to Mom.

Luckily, everyone seemed to be too focused on their own conversations.

Could no one else see it? Was I losing it? I stared at my glowing lunch box again. My heart beat faster. Should I open it? Who knew what could be creating that eerie yellow glow? What if there were aliens hiding out inside?

Eventually my curiosity got to me. I began to slowly unzip the lunch box.

If I get attacked by aliens, at least I'll be remembered for something cooler than being the kid who brought seaweed for lunch, I thought to myself.

I lifted one corner of my lunch box and peeked inside. As I did, the glow faded. My eyes widened, and I slammed the flap back down.

"Wait . . . that's not . . ." I whispered.

I lifted the top of my lunch box. I rubbed my eyes once. Then again. And again. No matter how hard I rubbed, what I saw didn't change. Instead of mandoo, a ham and cheese sandwich stared back at me.

I took the sandwich out of the baggie and poked it, checking to see if it was real. "What . . . b-but how . . . this morning . . ."

"Excuse me. Want me to throw that baggie away for you?" a voice asked.

I turned around and saw Mr. Wiz coming toward me with a garbage can.

"Sure . . . thank you . . ." I said, still in shock. What had happened to my lunch?

Mr. Wiz nodded and grabbed the empty baggie from my table before walking over to the next one.

I stared at my sandwich in awe. A quick look around the cafeteria told me it was nearly identical to the other kids' lunches. I couldn't believe it. My wish had come true!

I took a big bite of ham and cheese. It tasted pretty good. Maybe not as good as my mom's cooking, but at least no one was making fun of me.

How was this possible, though? I clearly remembered seeing mandoo in my lunch box that morning, and Mom had said that we didn't have any bread at home.

Had someone accidentally switched lunches with me? Was this some kind of joke? And if not, what was happening?

✦✦✦

"How was lunch today?" Mom asked when I got home.

I froze. "It was good."

It wasn't *really* a lie. Sure, I'd had a ham and cheese sandwich instead of mandoo, but it had been good. Or at least okay.

"Umma . . . can I ask you something?" I said.

Mom looked at me. "Sure, Ben. What is it?"

I took a deep breath. "Did you do something different to my lunch today?"

Her eyes widened. "Wow, Ben! I can't believe you noticed!"

Ha! So she *had* changed my lun—

"I used ground beef instead of pork this time!" Mom finished.

She looked so impressed that I didn't think it was a good time to correct her. Besides, she probably wouldn't believe me anyway. Who would?

CHAPTER 5

THE VOICE

The next day, I made sure to take a quick peek inside my lunch box before I put it in my cubby. Mom had packed jabchae today. I'd watched her do it. Sure enough, when I opened the lunch box, brown glass noodles with veggies and beef waited.

I groaned. Yesterday must have been some kind of mix-up.

I dug my pencil case out of my backpack. We had a spelling test today, and I was excited to use my new pencils. My halmoni had sent them all the way from Korea. They were super-special mechanical pencils with squishy little animals attached to the tops. My favorite was the one with a sloth.

But when I opened my pencil case, I saw four regular old wooden pencils. No cool animals, just yellow wood and pink erasers.

Why are these in here? I wondered.

I stuck my head into my backpack again and pushed past all the junk. I knew I'd put my new pencils in the case this morning.

A familiar voice interrupted my search. "Morning."

I looked up to see Mr. Wiz making his way down the hall. He leaned over to pick up a piece of paper from the floor. As he did, a necklace with an oval-shaped pendant swung free of his shirt. It glowed a bright yellow.

"I like your necklace," I said, pointing to it.

Mr. Wiz quickly tucked the necklace back into his shirt. His eyes crinkled at the corners. "Thanks, Ben," he said.

Then he grabbed the trash can and continued down the hall.

Wait. Ben? Did he say Ben? How did he know my name? I didn't remember ever telling him my name.

I whirled around. "Wait!" I called after him. But Mr. Wiz was already gone.

✦◆✦

I sat alone at lunch again that day. I was lonely, but I didn't want a repeat of the first day of school. And I couldn't risk anyone seeing my lunch box after what had happened yesterday.

Unless I just imagined it all, I thought.

But as soon as I reached for my lunch box, I saw the yellow glow. It was happening again!

Like yesterday, the glow around my lunch box grew bigger and brighter, lighting up the whole cafeteria. And just like yesterday, no one else seemed to notice. Was I the only person who could see what was happening?

I unzipped my lunch box. A peanut butter and jelly sandwich!

I grabbed the sandwich out of its baggie and bit into it. Not a bad sandwich, but not nearly as good as my mom's cooking. Thinking about her jabchae made my mouth water. I imagined the sweet, salty noodles mixed with beef, mushrooms, carrots, eggs, and spinach.

It would have been delicious, but at least no one was making fun of me.

Wait. I looked up. Not only was no one making fun of me . . . no one was paying attention to me—at all!

But I'm normal now! I thought. So why was I still alone?

All around me, other kids were enjoying lunch. A pair of younger kids flicked carrots across the cafeteria. Two boys shared jokes from a funny book. Shawn performed water bottle tricks for his friends.

The sandwich suddenly felt dry in my mouth. I put it down and looked over at the empty seats next to me. Nothing seemed to have changed from my first day at my new school.

Just then, I heard a faint voice from behind me. "Isn't this what you wanted?"

I spun my head around. I was sure I'd heard a voice. I scanned the area around me, but all I saw were students talking a couple tables away and Mr. Wiz wiping a table.

"Hello?" I whispered nervously. But no one answered.

CHAPTER 6

DISAPPEARING ACT

The next morning, I found Emilio waiting in front of my house.

"Hey, Ben!" he greeted me. "Want to walk to the bus stop together?" he asked.

"Sure," I said, looking around. "Where did you—"

Emilio smiled. "I live down the street." He pointed to a house a few doors down from mine.

We started for the bus stop at the corner. As we passed by Emilio's house, the front door swung open. A short woman with long brown hair stepped out.

“Emilio! Don’t forget to bring your sweatshirt back home, mijo,” she called.

“¡Sí, mamá!” Emilio yelled back.

My eyes widened. “You speak another language too?” I asked.

Emilio nodded. “Yep! Spanish. My parents are more comfortable with it. They came from Mexico when I was a baby,” he replied. “What about you?”

“I speak Korean,” I said.

"Cool! You should teach me some time," he said.

I thought quietly for a minute. Emilio and I had a lot in common. We both spoke different languages and had different cultures. I wondered if he ever had any of the same thoughts I did.

"Did you ever wish you weren't . . . different?" I finally asked.

Emilio stopped walking and looked at me. He tapped a finger on his chin like he was thinking hard.

"Sometimes," he finally replied. "When I first started at Andaleen, some kids thought the things I liked were weird—like the shows I watched or the food I brought to school. It bothered me at first, but then I realized they're just missing out. You know what I mean?"

I nodded. Emilio's experience sounded a lot like my first day at Andaleen, but I'd never thought about it like that. Like maybe everyone else was missing out.

✦◆✦

That morning in social studies, we learned about world history and geography. Ms. Bailey pointed out Asia on the world map.

I squinted, trying to find Korea. I knew exactly what it looked like because my mom always pointed it out on the globe.

"See this teeny tiny country?" she'd say. "The one that looks like a tiny boot cut in half? That's Korea!"

Ms. Bailey talked about the different parts of Asia—China, Japan, Vietnam. I kept waiting for her to say *Korea*. She kept going, naming Thailand, India, Indonesia.

Then she stopped. "And that's Asia!" she said. "There are a lot of other countries, but we won't be able to cover all of them in our unit."

"What about Korea?" I blurted out.

Ms. Bailey turned toward me. "Oh, Ben! I'm so glad you asked! You're from Korea, aren't you?" she asked.

I shook my head. "No, I'm not, but my parents are."

Mom and Dad had both been born in South Korea. They'd lived there most of their lives before moving to the United States. I'd only been to South Korea once, two years ago, to visit my grandma. The food was amazing, and we went to a lot of theme parks.

Ms. Bailey's face lit up. "Why don't you come show us where Korea is on the map?"

I hadn't expected her to call me up. But I knew exactly where Korea was, so I didn't feel too nervous.

I felt the stares on me as I walked up to the board. I took a deep breath and started searching for Korea.

The tiny boot. The tiny boot. The tiny boot, I repeated in my head.

I scanned the map, but I couldn't find Korea. It wasn't there. I felt sweat forming on my forehead. I knew where the country was *supposed* to be, but it was just . . . missing. It was as if someone had taken a big eraser and rubbed it off the map.

"Ben? It's okay if you're not sure," Ms. Bailey said quietly, putting a hand on my back.

"I-I forgot where it is," I whispered.

"That's okay. We all forget sometimes," Ms. Bailey said.

I nodded, feeling my face turning as red as a tomato as I walked back to my desk. Ms. Bailey continued teaching, but I couldn't stop staring at the map. What was happening to me?

CHAPTER 7

TV TROUBLE

When I got home, I stretched out on my bed, tossing a bouncy ball in the air. *Smmmmack! Smmmmmack!* I loved the sound it made when it fell back into my hand. I couldn't stop replaying the past few days in my head.

The switch had happened again at lunch. Chicken nuggets. I'd stuffed them back in my lunch box and put my head down for the rest of lunch. I was really starting to miss my mom's cooking.

Someone had to be switching out my lunch. But why? Was it some kind of prank?

And how did I explain the bright yellow glow? I had inspected my lunch box inside and out, but there were no hidden lights.

Thinking about it all made my brain hurt! Maybe watching TV would distract me. Our TV was extra cool—it played English and Korean shows. And today was Thursday, which meant that *Tobot V* would be on!

I went downstairs to the living room and flipped through the channels as fast as I could. Channel five, channel six, channel seven, channel eight, channel nine, channel . . . twenty?

What? That can't be right. Channels ten to nineteen were supposed to be the Korean channels.

I tried again. Channel twenty. Channel . . . nine? I kept flipping back and forth, but no matter what, there was nothing between nine and twenty.

What is happening? I thought. *Channels can't just disappear!*

I went back and forth about a hundred times before pressing the *off* button on the remote and tossing it to the side of the couch. I shoved my face into one of the pillows.

"Argh!!"

Mom stuck her head out from the kitchen. "Ben? Everything okay?" she asked. "Want a snack?"

"No thanks, Umma," I answered.

"Not watching *Tobot V* today?" Mom asked. She brought me an orange anyway and sat next to me on the couch.

I groaned. "No. It's not working."

"Not working? That can't be right." She grabbed the remote and started pressing buttons. I sulked back into my pillow.

"Here! It's on! See?" Mom pointed the remote at the screen.

I stared at the TV. A black screen stared back at me.

"There's nothing there," I said.

Mom ruffled my hair. "What do you mean? It's *Tobot V*, silly." She handed me the remote and walked back to the kitchen.

I rubbed my eyes. I pinched my arm. I even slapped myself on the cheek. There was absolutely nothing on the screen. It was blank—pure black.

"Ben! Dinner!" My mom yelled from downstairs later that evening.

I was still trying to make sense of why the TV hadn't worked earlier, but when I sniffed the air, I jumped off my bed. *Mmm.* Kalguksu!

"Coming!" I answered.

The yummy handmade noodles with seafood had been the most popular dish at my mom's restaurant. Just the thought of digging into her famous noodles made my mouth water.

I raced down the stairs and slid across the living room to the kitchen. Dad was already sitting at the table. He chuckled when he saw the excitement on my face.

"Looks like someone's ready to eat," Dad said.

"Yep!" I grabbed my chopsticks from one of the kitchen drawers.

"How was your day today?" Dad asked.

My face fell. "Fine," I lied, taking a seat next to him. "How was work?"

Dad laughed. "Well, if you think sitting in an office with your computer is fun, then I guess it was great."

Just then Mom came into the room carrying a steaming bowl of kalguksu. "Oh, stop," she said, setting it in front of me. Yummm.

“All right let’s hurry and eat before it gets cold,” Dad said, drumming his chopsticks on the table.

“Race you to finish the noodles first, Appa!” I shouted.

I used my chopsticks to scoop up a pile of noodles and shoved them into my mouth. I closed my eyes, preparing myself for the yummy seafood taste. But as soon as the noodles touched my tongue, a different taste filled my mouth. Spaghetti?

I looked down at the noodles in my bowl. They *looked* like kalguksu. The noodles were white, glistening with clear broth. There was absolutely no trace of tomato sauce.

I narrowed my eyes in Dad's direction. Was this another one of his jokes?

"Did you do something to my noodles?" I asked.

"Now you're just being a sore loser," Dad replied.

I watched as he continued shoveling noodles into his mouth. It didn't make any sense! I was sure the noodles had changed as soon as they entered my mouth.

I grabbed some more noodles with my chopsticks and slowly took a bite. Yup. It definitely tasted like spaghetti. Meatballs, tomato sauce, and all!

What had happened to my kalguksu? I chugged water, wiped my tongue, and took the tiniest of bites. But no matter what I did, the kalguksu still tasted like spaghetti.

I grumbled to myself as I ate more of the kalguksu-but-not-really-kalguksu. It wasn't that I didn't like spaghetti. I did. I was just really really *really* looking forward to the kalguksu.

After a couple more bites, I put my chopsticks down and scooted my bowl away. "Can I be excused?" I asked.

I must've looked sick because Mom put a hand on my forehead. "What's wrong, Ben? You barely ate."

"I'm not hungry," I mumbled.

"You usually ask for seconds!" she said. "Are you feeling okay?"

I pulled away. "I'm just not hungry, okay?"

I put my dish by the sink and ran up to my room. I didn't know what was going on, but I knew something was wrong—*very* wrong.

CHAPTER 8

THE CALL

The next day in class, we worked on cover pages for our fiction stories. Mine was about a superhero who was also part dinosaur.

As I started drawing out the main character, my mind drifted back to dinner the night before. When I looked down at my paper a few minutes later, I was shocked to see I had doodled a drawing of evil spaghetti!

I looked over at the other students. Some kids, including Angie, were working in a group. I remembered her asking me to sit with her at lunch. I really wished I'd said yes. Lunch would be a lot more fun if I had someone to sit with.

With a groan, I put my head on my desk.

A few minutes later, Ms. Bailey knelt by my desk. "Ben? Is everything okay?"

Ugh, not again, I thought, remembering my last conversation with her. It had made me feel more frustrated instead of less. I picked my head up off my desk.

"I just have a headache," I mumbled.

She didn't look too convinced. "Why don't you go to the nurse's office?"

"Okay," I replied.

I stood up and made my way out of the classroom. As I went, I thought about everything that had happened the past few days. The mysterious lunch box. The missing Korean TV channels. The changed noodles. None of it made any sense!

Suddenly, a quiet voice interrupted my thoughts.

"So, Ben, is this what you wanted?"

I felt my breath stop. That question sounded so familiar. I turned and saw Mr. Wiz standing there. His gray beard glistened like silver in the hallway light. I noticed his necklace was tucked into his shirt today. I wanted to ask him about it, but I didn't want to be nosy.

"Wh-what do you mean?" I asked. Did the custodian know something?

Mr. Wiz chuckled. "You dropped this," he said, holding up a piece of Korean green-grape candy. It must've fallen out of my pocket. Mom always had a bag of them, and I liked to sneak a few.

My shoulders relaxed. "Oh, I guess so. Thank you, Mr. Wiz," I replied.

I took the candy from him and stuck it back in my pocket. I was a little afraid to eat it. What if it tasted like chocolate or something else it wasn't supposed to?

Mr. Wiz smiled and leaned against his mop. "Good! Glad to hear it," he said. "So how do you like Andaleen so far?"

"It's fine," I said.

Mr. Wiz looked around, then signaled for me to come closer. "Now, I'll let you in on a little secret," he whispered. "Some people say strange things sometimes happen to the new students here."

I froze. "Wh-what do you mean?"

Mr. Wiz rubbed his beard thoughtfully. "I heard they turn new students into . . ." He paused. "The friendliest kids ever! Looks like it's already happened to you!"

I smiled. "Right," I said quietly.

Mr. Wiz winked, then grabbed his mop again. "Good to see you, Ben. You'd better get going, though. Wouldn't want you to lose anything else important."

Ring! Ring! Riiiiing!

I heard my mom run to the kitchen and answer the phone. "Jal-ji-nae-ji-yo? I hope you're doing well," she said. There was a moment of silence, then, "Ben! Come downstairs and say hello to Halmoni!"

I jumped up. I loved my grandma's weekly phone calls. She always told the funniest Korean folktales, like the one about the frog that did the opposite of everything his mom said. She also made the best Korean food. It was even better than Mom's, but I would *never* tell her that.

"Coming, Umma!" I yelled back. I skipped down the stairs.

Mom was waiting for me. "Don't forget to thank Halmoni for the pencils she sent you," she reminded me.

I gulped. I still couldn't find the pencils, but I decided it would be better if I didn't bring that up. It would probably make Halmoni sad.

I grabbed the phone. "Halmoni! How are you?" I asked in Korean.

All I heard on the other end was a jumble of static. It sounded like a broken radio.

"Grandma?" I heard the strange noises again. I shook the phone a few times. Maybe it was broken.

"Umma! Something's wrong with the phone!" I handed it to her. "It keeps making weird sounds."

Mom put the phone to her ear. "Yeo-bo-sae-yo? Hello?" she said. She was quiet for a moment, then looked at me strangely. "Okay, I'll tell him."

"It's broken, isn't it?" I asked.

Mom handed the phone back to me. "She says she was talking to you, but you didn't respond."

"B-but she didn't say anything!" I protested. "Really! It was just a weird mumble jumble of sounds!"

I put the phone back to my ear. "Sorry, Halmoni! Something weird was going on with Mom's phone."

I waited for a response, but the strange noises were still there. I couldn't understand a single thing.

"Halmoni . . . ?"

That's when a horrible realization swept over me. Lunch. My pencils. The map of Korea. *Tobot V*. The noodles. And now . . .

"No way."

The phone dropped from my hands. I couldn't breathe. The room spun around me like I was being sucked into a black hole. This couldn't be happening. I couldn't understand Halmoni!

Mom hurried over. "Ben. Ben? Ben! What's wrong with you?"

I looked at my mom's confused face. *Sorry, Umma*. I wanted to explain, but I couldn't.

I ran across the kitchen and bolted out the front door.

"I can't do this anymore. I just want things to go back to normal!" I cried.

A tear rolled down my cheek. Soon messy globs of snot and tears covered my face. All I wanted was to hear my grandma's voice. All I wanted was to talk to her.

I shook my head. I couldn't stand around crying like this. I couldn't just let this happen. I had to do something. I had to fix this.

CHAPTER 9

EMILIO'S SECRET

I spent most of the weekend in my room, trying to think. I needed to come up with some sort of plan.

Will I ever be able to talk to Halmoni again? I worried.

At lunch on Monday, I picked at my turkey and cheese sandwich. My appetite was gone—just like Halmoni.

Suddenly, loud voices erupted at a nearby table.

"Emilio, what is THAT?"

"Is that mud?"

"That smells like barf."

I turned away from my glowing lunch box to see a group of kids crowded around Emilio. Everyone was pointing at his food. I shrank in my seat. It felt like the kimbap incident on my first day. My stomach churned remembering it.

But to my surprise, Emilio laughed.

"Are you kidding me?" he said. "This is mole and rice! You guys are seriously telling me you've never had it before?"

I watched as Emilio scooped up a massive spoonful and scarfed it down in one bite.

"Deeeeelicious!" he declared. "You guys have to try some."

The other kids exchanged confused looks. Finally, one of the boys shrugged and grabbed Emilio's spoon. He scooped some of the mole and rice and took a small bite.

"Hmm . . . a little spicy but good," he said.

"See! What did I tell ya?" Emilio gave him a friendly slap on the back.

Kids started to gather around Emilio's table.

"I wanna try it! I wanna try it!"

"How spicy is it?"

"What does it taste like?"

Emilio didn't look even the tiniest bit annoyed that everyone was eating his lunch. Instead, he leaned back in his seat, crossed his arms, and grinned confidently.

I thought back to my first day of school and the embarrassment I'd felt when the kids had pointed at my lunch. I looked back at Emilio's confident smile. How did he do it?

Just then, Emilio looked over at me—at my lunch box, to be exact. He gave me a knowing wink before turning back toward his friends.

My jaw dropped. That could only mean one thing—Emilio saw the glow.

I sat in my usual spot on the bus, looking out the window. I couldn't get Emilio's wink out of my head. No one else had been able to see the bright glow from my lunch box. So how could he?

I was so lost in thought that I jumped when I heard a voice. "Happening to you too, huh?"

I looked up to see Emilio sliding into the seat next to me. "Wh-what do you mean?" I stammered.

Emilio shook his head. "The lunch box? The glow? The magic?" He waved his hands around like he was doing a magic trick.

"You could see it!"

"Oh, I could see it, all right. It's kind of hard to miss." He laughed. "I remember the first time it happened to me."

I couldn't have heard him right. "What do you mean, the first time it happened to you?"

Emilio leaned back in his seat. "When I moved here in third grade, I was the only Mexican kid at the school. I brought pozole, and everyone said it looked disgusting." He frowned, like he was remembering that exact moment.

"Anyway, the next day, there was this crazy yellow glow," he continued. "Then, *BAM*! My lunch changed from tamales to a sandwich! I thought I was losing it, but it kept happening over and over and over."

"That's exactly what happened to me!" I gasped. "How did your lunch go back to normal?"

"After the kids made fun of my pozole, I ended up hiding my lunch box in a bush," Emilio answered. "After days of missing Mexican food, I went back and found it again. I took it home and everything went back to normal!"

I thought back to my first day. I'd thrown away my *Tobot V* lunch box and had been forced to start bringing the boring blue one.

"What did you do with your lunch box?" Emilio asked. "You had that cool robot one on the first day of school."

I hung my head sadly. "I threw it away. I'm sure it's long gone now."

"Well, you're going to need it," Emilio said. "I think I know how you can get it back . . . but you're not going to like it."

CHAPTER 10

OPERATION LUNCH BOX

The next morning, Emilio and I hurried off the bus and straight to the cafeteria. We had decided to get there first thing. That way no one else would be in there.

Hurry, hurry, hurry, I chanted silently. I couldn't be late for class. I huffed and puffed as we turned the corner. *Almost there.*

We screeched to a halt in front of the cafeteria. It looked strange without any kids eating lunch. The lights were off, and the only sound was our footsteps.

Once we were inside, I turned to Emilio. "What's the plan?"

"You're not going to like it . . ." he warned me again.

"I'll do anything!" I said.

I hadn't realized how much my Korean culture meant to me until it disappeared. The food, shows, country, and language were such a big part of who I was. I was determined to get it back, no matter what it took.

Emilio made a face. "Remember how I said things went back to normal once I got my lunch box back? I think you need to do the same. Unfortunately . . . you threw yours in the garbage can." He pointed across the cafeteria.

I followed Emilio's finger. "The garbage can? You must be joking. There's no way it's still in there," I argued. "I threw it away days ago."

But Emilio didn't look like he was joking. His arms were crossed, and his lips were pressed firmly together.

I walked over to the garbage can and peeked in. The smell was horrible—a mix of rotten eggs, sour pickles, and old milk. I held my breath, trying not to gag.

"There has to be another way," I said. There was no way I was going to go in there!

Emilio shrugged. "I said you weren't going to like it."

I was about to turn away . . . then I thought about my phone call with Halmoni. The way her words had jumbled into meaningless sounds. If there was a chance I could fix things—any chance at all—I had to try.

I clenched my fists and faced Emilio. "Let's get this over with."

Emilio's lips curved into a smile. "Okay, then!"

I pinched my nose with my left hand and stuck my right hand into the garbage can. Wrappers, slimy leftover food, and plastic utensils slipped through my fingers.

I gagged as I rooted around in the trash. "Emilio . . . you . . . better . . . be . . . right . . . about . . . this!" I stuck my head in to get a better look. "Where is it?"

Suddenly a ray of bright yellow light flashed before my eyes. *Zwooooop!* Before I had time to pull away, a powerful force sucked my whole body into the garbage can!

"Ahhhhh!" I screamed, forgetting that it probably wasn't the best idea to open my mouth inside a garbage can.

Trash flew past as the force sucked me in deeper. I should have hit the bottom of the garbage can after two seconds, but I kept falling. I felt like I was on a roller coaster that dropped forever.

Another bright ray of light flashed in front of me, and I covered my eyes with both hands, preparing for the worst.

Then, suddenly . . . *bam!* My bottom hit something hard. A roar of noise surrounded me. It was almost deafening. I heard people talking around me.

"I think I might be the best soccer player on my team."

"Ally said she didn't want to be Erica's friend anymore!"

"Don't forget to meet us at the tree during recess!"

I'd heard those same words before. I spread my fingers out, just the tiniest bit, to try to see where I was. Tables, kids, lunch boxes . . . lunch boxes?!

I ripped my hands away from my eyes. In front of me were rows of long tables. Each one was filled with kids, all chatting away as they ate lunch.

I was back in the cafeteria. How?

Before I could figure out what was happening, Shawn walked over with two of his friends. He stared at me for a moment, then looked away and sat down a few seats away. He immediately began bragging to his friends about how many monsters he'd defeated in his game yesterday.

I looked around the cafeteria again, and that's when I realized there was something on the table in front of me. In front of me was . . . my *Tobot V* lunch box?

I grabbed the lunch box with both hands. I slowly turned it around. Written on the back in permanent marker was my name. Ben Lee.

I set it back down on the table and unzipped the lunch box. No yellow glow. That was a good sign. I flipped open the cover, and my eyes widened.

"Kimbap!" I shouted, jumping up from my seat.

All around me, kids turned to stare. Oops. I hadn't meant to say that so loudly. I felt my cheeks warm as I sat back down in my seat.

"What's that?" someone asked.

I looked up to see Shawn scooting closer. *Oh, great.*

"It's kimbap," I replied.

"Kim-what?" Shawn asked.

Wait. This sounded too familiar. I scooted away a little and stared at Shawn. He was wearing a bright green shirt with an alien face on the front. I recognized it. It was the same one he'd been wearing on my first day.

"Hello! Earth to Ben! Is that your lunch? What's that black stuff?" Shawn scrunched up his nose.

I definitely recognized *that* face. This was a repeat of my first day! I saw kids gathering around, pointing at my kimbap and whispering.

I looked at my lunch box. My heart was beating fast. I thought about everything that had happened.

I thought about how my mom woke up early every morning to make my lunch fresh. I thought about how much I had missed her Korean cooking. I thought about how Emilio had stood up to the other kids when they made fun of his mole and rice.

I took a deep breath. "It's seaweed," I said, keeping my voice as steady as possible. "And it's a part of kimbap, my favorite food in the whole world."

I pulled apart my wooden chopsticks, picked up a piece of kimbap, and popped it in my mouth. The kids gasped.

"What is that?"

"He said it's seaweed!"

"Why would he eat seaweed?"

"That smells kinda weird."

"Are you sure that's even food?"

I refused to let their comments get to me. "Did you know that there are ten different ingredients in kimbap? It takes more than two hours to make."

I looked each kid in the eye. I'm sure my hands were shaking, but I didn't care.

"My mom made these," I continued. "She had her own restaurant in California. Maybe you should try it first before saying anything about it."

The kids around me were quiet. From the corner of my eye, I spotted Shawn rubbing the back of his neck. He cleared his throat.

"Sorry, Ben. You're right," he said.

Did he just apologize? I couldn't believe it.

For a minute, I was still upset. It made me sad and mad to think about the other kids making fun of my lunch. But Shawn's apology seemed genuine.

I took another deep breath. "What you did wasn't okay," I said. Then I smiled. "But I forgive you."

Shawn smiled back. "Thanks," he said. He pointed at the kimbap in my container. "Hey, do you think I could try one?"

I couldn't believe it. "Sure!" I replied, reaching for my chopsticks.

As soon as my fingers touched them, a flash of light blinded me again.

Zwoooop! Bam!

CHAPTER 11

CONNECTING THE DOTS

I felt my bottom hit something hard—again. But this time, the rotten smell of leftover food filled the air around me.

"P.U.!" I spat.

I looked around. I was back in the garbage can for sure.

I wiggled around, trying to get out, but the garbage can barely budged. The smell was awful. I had to get out. I pushed against one side as hard as I could, and the garbage can tipped, then crashed against the floor.

"I made it!" I shouted, crawling free. "I'm alive!" I pumped my fists in the air.

Emilio stood in front of me, grinning. "You did it!" He moved to give me a hug but stopped himself when he got a better look at me. "Maybe the hug can wait."

"I was . . . I went back to . . . it was the first . . . I think I just time traveled!" I managed to spit out.

Emilio shook his head. "Yep. Sounds about right," he said. "Same thing happened to me."

I had about a million questions, but before I could ask any of them, I heard the squeak of wheels rolling on the floor. Emilio and I frantically looked for a place to hide, but it was too late. The lights in the cafeteria switched on.

"Emilio? Ben?" Mr. Wiz stood in the doorway with his mop bucket. "What are you two doing in the cafeteria at this time

of the day?" He rubbed a hand against his temple, puzzled.

I looked at Emilio for help. "Uh . . . about that . . . I just . . . came to look for something."

Emilio bent over and grabbed my *Tobot V* lunch box from the floor. He held it up in the air.

"He was looking for this!" Emilio added.

Mr. Wiz eyed us suspiciously for a minute. "Is that so?"

Emilio and I both nodded.

"Well, I don't think you can go back to class like *that*," Mr. Wiz finally said, pointing at my messy shirt. "You get some different clothes from the office. I'll write you notes to give to your teachers."

Mr. Wiz reached into his back pocket and pulled out a pack of sticky notes and a pen. He scribbled furiously.

As he leaned over to write, I caught a glimpse of his necklace again. It was glowing a bright yellow, just like it had before. The glow. It reminded me of . . . my lunch box.

Before I could ask him about it, Mr. Wiz handed Emilio and me each a sticky note.

"All right now, hurry along! Your teachers are going to wonder where you've been!" said Mr. Wiz.

"Thank you," we both said and dashed out of the cafeteria.

✦◆✦

After going to the office to get clean clothes, I hurried back to my classroom. I carefully placed my lunch box into my backpack before entering the room. Everyone else was already at their desks.

"Ben, you're late," Ms. Bailey said.

"Sorry," I said, trying to keep my voice calm. "I . . . uh . . . I was helping Mr. Wiz."

I reached into my pocket for the note from Mr. Wiz. I was about to hand it over when I saw what it said: *Check inside your lunch box.*

I quickly pulled the note away. Ms. Bailey blinked.

"Uh . . . this isn't it," I said quickly. "I must've lost the pass. Sorry. Again."

"Okay, just take your seat," Ms. Bailey told me.

I breathed a sigh of relief and sat down.

"*Pssst!*" Angie hissed from her desk across the aisle.

"What?" I whispered.

"Can I borrow a pencil?" Angie whispered back to me.

"Sure."

I took out my pencil case. When I opened it, I *gasped*. The mechanical pencils from Halmoni were inside!

"Here," I said proudly, pulling out one with a squishy polar bear on top.

"Whoa! This is such a cool pencil!" Angie said. She used it to write her name on her paper.

"Thanks," I replied with a proud smile. "I know."

✦◆✦

As soon as the lunch bell rang, I grabbed my backpack. I couldn't stop thinking about Mr. Wiz's note. *Check inside your lunch box.*

Why would he write that? What did it mean?

I carefully unzipped my lunch box. Even before I opened it all the way, I knew what was inside. I would recognize that smell anywhere. I flipped open the cover of the lunch box as fast as I could and grabbed the container inside. Kimbap!

"Yes! It's back!" I shouted, lifting my lunch box in the air.

"What's that?" Angie interrupted my thoughts.

I hesitated. "Oh, this? It's . . ." Then I remembered standing up to the kids who'd made fun of my lunch. I pushed my lunch box toward Angie. "This is kimbap. My mom made it."

"What's in it?" Angie asked.

"It's actually ten different ingredients!" I exclaimed. "Seaweed, ground beef, pickled radish, and all kinds of vegetables . . ."

"Mmmm! That sounds yummy!" Angie replied.

I looked at my kimbap, then back at her. "Do you maybe want to sit by me at lunch?" I fidgeted with the lunch box zipper.

"Of course!" Angie said.

I grinned. For the first time in a long time, I couldn't wait for lunch.

CHAPTER 12

THE FINAL TEST

I ran all the way home from the bus stop. Eating with Angie today had been so much fun. She'd even tried kimbap—and loved it! I couldn't wait to sit with her again tomorrow.

"Umma! I'm home!" I shouted, throwing open the front door.

Mom came out of the kitchen, and I threw my arms around her.

"Well, hi, Ben! You're in a good mood today, aren't you?" Mom said, squeezing me back. "How was your—" She froze. "What happened to your clothes?"

"Oh, I-I . . ." I had to think of something! "I fell in the mud at recess," I quickly finished.

Mom tsked. "How many times have I told you to watch out for the mud?" she asked.

I rolled my eyes. At least it was better than telling her I'd gone digging through the garbage can today.

That reminded me . . . if my lunch box was back to normal, did that mean everything else was too? I had to find out. I turned and ran to the living room.

"Whoa, Ben! What's the rush?" Mom asked, following me.

I grabbed the remote and clicked away. *Please, please, please!*

I stopped on a channel. The five seconds it took to load felt like five days. Finally . . . *ding!* A cartoon car appeared on the screen, and a familiar theme song began to play.

"*Tobot V*!" I danced around the living room, shouting the words to the theme song.

My mom laughed. "What's gotten into you, Ben?"

I stopped dancing and caught my breath. Then I turned to my mom. "Can we have kalguksu for dinner? And can I call Halmoni? Oh, and where's the globe? I need to see the globe!"

"Calm down, Ben. The globe is in the basement. I'll go make kalguksu. But don't leave half of it uneaten like last time," Mom warned.

I nodded and raced down to the basement to dig through boxes.

"Gotta find the globe," I said. Finally, I spotted it. I grabbed the globe and started searching for Korea. "The tiny boot. Find the tiny boot."

My finger glided across China and stopped. The tiny boot cut in half. Korea. It was really there.

"I found it!" I yelled.

I ran back upstairs and spent the rest of the afternoon watching *Tobot V*. I had missed my favorite show so much.

Finally, Dad came home from work, and Mom called to us from the kitchen. "Dinner's ready!"

I ran to the table. A delicious-looking bowl of kalguksu waited for me.

Taking a deep breath, I sat down and brought a chopstick-full of noodles to my mouth. *Slurp! Yummm!* The chewy noodles and seafood broth filled my mouth. It was kalguksu, all right. Thank goodness!

We had just finished eating when Mom's phone rang.

"Ben, can you get the phone?" Mom asked. She and Dad were busy clearing the table.

I gulped when I saw Halmoni's name on the phone. Everything else had turned back to normal, but the most important was my grandma.

"Okay," I replied.

I walked slowly over to the phone. My hands shook as I picked it up. I pressed the answer button and took a deep breath as I put the phone against my ear and braced myself.

"Yeo-bo-sae-yo? Hello?" I answered.

"Ben-ah? Is that you?" a warm voice replied in Korean.

I felt my eyes fill with tears. "Halmoni!"

My grandma wasted no time. She immediately asked why I couldn't hear her the other day. I told her it was a long story. Then I told her about my new school and the newest episode of *Tobot V*. My grandma told me about the new bakery she wanted to take me to next time I visited Korea. She also made sure to tell me the frog story.

We talked and talked and talked until we ran out of things to talk about.

"I have to go now, Ben-ya," my grandma told me.

"Halmoni, can I talk to you tomorrow too?" I asked.

My grandma chuckled. "Of course. Saranghae."

"I love you too," I replied.

After we hung up, I looked over at my mom. There was just one more thing I had to do.

"Umma, can you pack kimbap again for lunch tomorrow?" I asked.

"Again? You just had it a few days ago," she said.

"Yeah . . ." I said. "But it's my favorite!"

GLOSSARY

appa (ah-PA)—Korean word for dad

daze (DEYZ)—the state of being stunned

grimace (GRIM-uhs)—a facial expression of disgust, disapproval, or pain

halmoni (hal-MOH-nee)—Korean word for grandmother

mole (MOH-ley)—a spicy sauce used in Mexican cooking and typically flavored with dark chocolate, chili peppers, and spices

pendant (PEN-duhnt)—something that hangs down, such as a decoration on a necklace

pickled (PIK-uhld)—preserved in brine or another liquid

pozole (poh-SOH-ley)—a thick soup from Mexico and the U.S. Southwest made with pork, hominy, garlic, and chili

proverb (PROV-erb)—a short saying that expresses a truth or offers advice

saranghae (sa-RAHNG-hae)—Korean phrase meaning, "I love you"

umma (uhm-MA)—Korean word for mom

yeo-bo-sae-yo (YEO-bo-sae-yo)—Korean phrase meaning, "Hello?" (usually said over the phone)

KOREAN FOODS

bibimbap (bee-buhm-BAAP)—a mixture of rice, vegetables, beef, egg, sesame oil, and red pepper paste

bulgogi (bul-GOW-gee)—sweet and salty slices of grilled beef

jabchae (chaap-CHAY)—stir-fried glass noodles with vegetables and beef

kalbi (KAL-bee)—barbequed beef short ribs

kalguksu (KAL-guk-soo)—knife-cut noodles in clear broth with seafood

kimbap (KEEM-bap)—a dish made from cooked rice, vegetables, fish, and meat rolled in a layer of seaweed and served in bite-size pieces

kimchi jjigae (KIM-chee JEE-gay)—spicy kimchi stew with pork or seafood and vegetables

mandoo (man-DOO)—dumplings filled with meat and vegetables

naengmyun (NAENG-myun)—cold noodles with chopped radish, chopped cucumber, egg, meat, and seasoned with vinegar and Korean mustard

soondoobu jjigae (soon-DOO-boo JEE-gay)—soft tofu stew with egg and clams

tteokbokki (tuk-bow-kee)—spicy sliced rice cakes cooked with fish cakes in spicy chili sauce

MAKE YOUR OWN KIMBAP

Mom's kimbap takes more than two hour to make! But you can try making your own using this simplified recipe. (It will make two rolls.) Ask an adult to help you with the shopping. You might need to visit an Asian market for some items.

Tools:

- rice cooker or saucepan
- vegetable peeler
- sharp knife
- skillet or sauté pan
- mixing bowl
- whisk
- skillet
- kimbap bamboo mat

Ingredients:

- 2 sheets of kim (seaweed)
- 2 cups of cooked rice
- 1 cup of ground beef*
- 2 strips of danmuji (yellow pickled radish)
- 1 small carrot, cut into thin strips
- 1 egg
- 4-5 ounces of spinach (blanched)
- 1/2 teaspoon of salt
- 1 tablespoon of sesame oil

*If you don't eat red meat, you could also use ground chicken or ground turkey.

What to Do:

Some of these steps might require an adult's help. Make sure you have someone willing to help before you start cooking.

1. Use a rice cooker or saucepan to cook rice according to package directions. (You can also buy cooked rice at the store.)
2. Mix freshly cooked rice with salt and sesame oil. Set aside and let cool.
3. Peel the carrot and use a sharp knife to cut it into strips. Then, sauté carrot strips in a skillet on the stove. (Ask an adult to help you with this step.)
4. Season ground beef with salt and pepper. Using the same skillet from step #3, cook the meat fully.
5. Crack egg into a mixing bowl and use a whisk to beat. Pour into a skillet and cook until firm. (Ask an adult to help before using the stove.) Cut the cooked egg into thin strips.
6. Lay kim sheets (shiny sheet down) on bamboo mat.
7. Spread a thin layer of cooked rice on the kim sheets, leaving only a little strip uncovered near the edge of the mat.
8. Place carrot strips, beef, egg strips, and spinach at the center of the rice.
9. Use both hands to tightly roll the bamboo mat. (Your ingredients should be rolled up inside.)
10. Once the kimbap is fully rolled, cut into bite-size circular pieces. Enjoy eating!

TALK ABOUT IT

1. How do you think Ben felt on his first day at Andaleen Elementary? What clues in the story help show how he's feeling? Talk about how you would feel if you were in Ben's position.

2. Mr. Wiz showed up multiple times throughout this story. What do you think his role was in the lunch switcheroos? Talk about your theories.

3. At the end of the story, Ben realizes he is proud of his Korean culture. What do you think contributed to his change of heart? What's something about yourself that you are proud of?

WRITE ABOUT IT

1. Emilio reveals to Ben that he went through a similar experience after starting at Andaleen Elementary. Imagine his first day. Write a short story about how Emilio might have reacted when his lunch changed for the first time.

2. Ben felt embarrassed when other kids made comments about his lunch. Have you ever been in a situation where you felt embarrassed? Write about what happened and how you dealt with it.

3. Imagine you are Ben. Write a letter to Halmoni explaining why you couldn't understand her the last time she called.

ABOUT THE AUTHOR

Photo credit: Milan Puscas

Hanna Kim is a children's book author and middle school English language arts teacher. Just like Ben, she was made fun of for her Korean lunches, and it took her some time to be proud of her culture. In her free time, Hanna loves to draw, read, make fun crafts, and eat Korean snacks. She lives in Michigan with her husband, Benjamin, and cat, Zoro.

ABOUT THE ILLUSTRATOR

Emily Paik is an illustrator who lives in South Korea with two dogs, Tofu and Doona. She loves to go on adventures with her dogs and gets inspired by the colors and shapes of nature. She hopes to create illustrations that will warm people's hearts and make them smile.

Photo credit: Emily Paik